PICTURE BOOK STUDIO USA

BIRD
ADALBERT

Susi Bohdal
Andrew Elborn

Bird Adalbert looked rather dowdy and plain,
But in spite of this fact, he was still rather vain.
He pouted and sulked, and he said with a frown,
"Why do I have to have feathers of brown?"

"I should be special – I want them to know
That I'm the top bird wherever I go!"
So he wished and he grumbled with all of his might –
All morning, all afternoon, straight through the night!

And here's where the story really begins,
For his wishing was heard by the Magical Twins.
They appeared by his tree at dawn the next day
And they listened again while the bird had his say.
Then they smiled two smiles and they blinked with four eyes,
And said, "First you'll be pretty, and then you'll be wise."

So the Twins cast a spell with a magical word,
And Adalbert changed to a beautiful bird!
His feathers were lovely, all bright bluish green,
And his head became red with a silvery sheen.

He said, "Now I'm handsome!" and puffed out his chest.
"I'm finally certain that I am the best!"

"You pigeons should bow when I come around –
  You know, stop all your cooing and scratching the ground…
  Show some respect for a beautiful bird:
  I am the most handsome – haven't you heard?"

The pigeons all looked, but, of course, no one bowed.
They went back to their cooing, just a big, happy crowd.

"You geese were made exactly wrong:
You're far too large with necks too long.
Now, I am made exactly right,
With lovely colors, perfect height.
It must be hard to be so drab –
No wonder all you do is gab!"

The downy geese just smiled at him,
Then waddled off to take a swim.

"Chickens! such an ugly group!
If I were one, I'd fly the coop!
Scratch and peck and peck and scratch –
Why do their eggs even bother to hatch?"

Adalbert's voice was loud and clear,
But the hen just pretended not to hear.

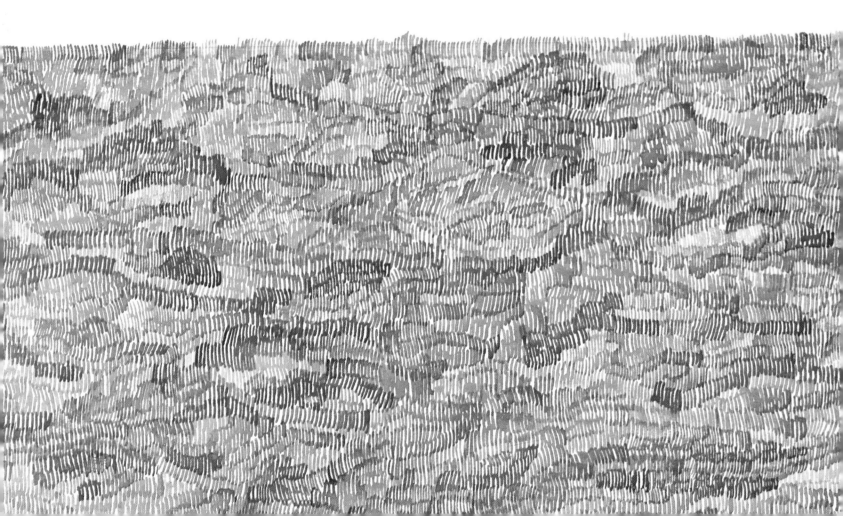

"It must be dull to be all black
On head and tail and front and back.
And then, as if that weren't enough,
Your creaky, croaky voice is rough!
Perhaps someone could make you coats
And tell you how to cure your throats.
Just think how happy you would be
If you could look and sound like me!"

The handsome ravens shared their limb,
But no one said one word to him

Aha! what's this down on the ground?
Four little lumps of dirty brown!
You silly sparrows are so small,
Why, I'm not sure you're there at all.
With all your hopping, chirping noise,
You might as well be wind-up toys.
You must be thrilled to look at me –
It's quite a treat; don't you agree?"

The little friends just hopped away
And went on with their busy day.

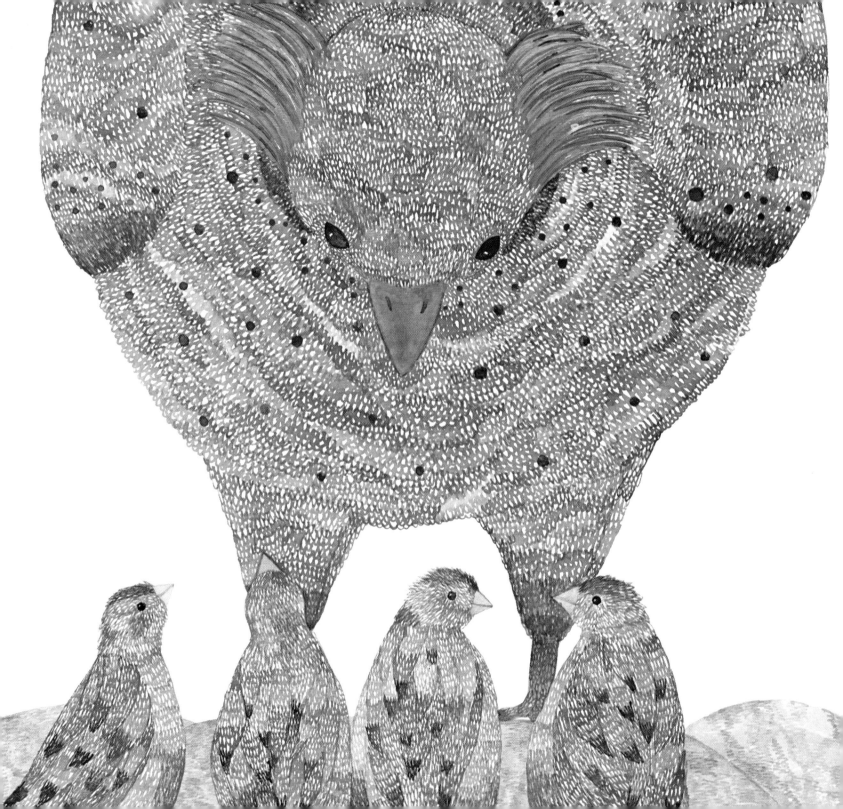

The owls had heard of Adalbert
And all the feelings he had hurt.
They listened while he made his jokes,
And then the largest blinked, and spoke:

"We have seen you in our dream.
We know where your pride will end:
However happy you may seem,
No one can live without a friend."

They stared at him with yellow eyes
And saw right through his bright disguise.

The owls were right: he lost his friends,
And he felt too proud to make amends.
So he stared at the moon, and he blinked at the sun
And pretended that being a hermit was fun.

One morning the Magical Twins came along,
And he told them how all of his plans had gone wrong.
Then he asked for their help – as he had once before –
And he promised he wouldn't be proud anymore.

"Our spell has worked: it's made you wise."
And they smiled two smiles and blinked four eyes.

Then the Twins said the magical word that they say,
And Adalbert's feeling of pride drained away!

He looked very different, and he felt different, too;
And he knew in a flash what he wanted to do.

He gave a little party, and invited all the birds.
He said, "I'm very sorry now for all those unkind words.
I really wouldn't blame you if you all just flew away."
The raven said, "It's clear you've changed... we'd really like to stay!"

There's only one more thing to say before the story ends:
Bright feathers may be pretty, but they're not as nice as friends.

Library of Congress Cataloging in Publication Data
Bohdal, Susi.
Bird Adalbert.
(Picture Book Studio USA)
Translation of: Der schöne Vogel Adalbert.
Summary: When Adalbert's wish for great beauty suddenly
comes true, he becomes so proud and overbearing with the
other birds that he is left alone and unhappy.
[1. Wishes–Fiction. 2. Beauty, Personal–Fiction.
3. Pride and vanity–Fiction. 4. Birds–Fiction]
I. Clements, Andrew, 1949-   . II. Title.